# H·E·B read 3

## GROW YOUNG MINDS, READ 3 TIMES A WEEK

H-E-B is strongly committed to improving education in Texas and has supported Texas schools through the Excellence in Education Awards program for more than 10 years. In 2011, when H-E-B learned that Texas was facing a major challenge regarding early childhood education and kindergarten readiness, H-E-B started the Read 3 Early Childhood Literacy Campaign.

Read 3's goals are to provide easy and affordable access to books for Texas families and encourage families to read to their early learners at least three times every week. Reading to a child improves his literacy, and when a child's literacy improves, she is more likely to succeed in school, less likely to drop out, and more likely to finish college. That's a brighter future for the child, the family, and for Texas.

**Commit to reading at least three times a week to your early learner. Take the Read 3 Pledge!**

"A, B, C and 1, 2, 3 – Reading is fun for me.
It helps me grow my young mind.
This week I pledge to read 3 times!"

# H·E·B read 3

H-E-B está firmemente comprometido a mejorar la educación en Texas y ha apoyado a las escuelas de Texas a través del programa de Premios a la Excelencia en la Educación por más de 10 años. En 2011, cuando H-E-B se enteró de que Texas enfrentaba un desafío importante con respecto a la educación de la infancia temprana y la preparación para el jardín de niños, H-E-B comenzó la Campaña de Alfabetización de la Infancia Temprana de Read 3.

Los objetivos de Read 3 son proporcionar un acceso fácil y asequible a los libros para las familias de Texas y alentar a las familias a que lean a sus estudiantes que están en la infancia temprana por al menos tres veces a la semana. Leerle a un niño mejora su alfabetización y cuando la alfabetización de un niño mejora, es más probable que tenga éxito en la escuela, menos probabilidades de abandonarla y más probabilidades de terminar la universidad. Ese es un futuro más brillante para el niño, la familia y para Texas.

**Comprométase a leer al menos tres veces por semana a su estudiante que está en la infancia temprana. ¡Tome la promesa de Read 3!**

"A, B, C y 1, 2, 3 - La lectura es divertida para mí. Me ayuda a desarrollar mi mente joven. ¡Esta semana me comprometo a leer 3 veces!"

# Disney

## This book belongs to

_____

# DISNEP

## THE
# SORCERER'S
## APPRENTICE

Long ago there lived a wise sorcerer. He had a tall, special hat that gave him amazing powers. All he had to do was *think* magic thoughts and they would come true. If he thought of a butterfly, out of nowhere, beautiful colors would swirl into shape and take flight. And with the sorcerer's secret words, the magic would end. Poof!

The sorcerer had an apprentice—a young helper—who did work for him around the castle. He swept the floor, he chopped the wood, and he carried water from the fountain down to the well in the cellar. It was hard work.

*If only I had that hat!* thought the apprentice. *I could just think my work into being done!*

One day, the sorcerer had to go out. He left his hat on a table in the cellar, deep in the castle where the apprentice was working.

The apprentice watched him go. This was his chance . . . .

"Now *I* can be a great sorcerer!" he said, as he put the hat onto his head.

Next to some water buckets, an old broom
stood against the wall. The apprentice eyed
that broom and began to wonder . . . and
imagine. He did what the sorcerer always
did. He pointed his fingers at the broom and
thought even harder.

All at once, the broom began to glow! Then
it began to move!

"Broom, pick up the buckets!" the apprentice ordered.

The broom grew arms! Each arm picked up a bucket!

"Follow me!" commanded the apprentice, leading the broom up the cellar steps.

The broom followed!

"To the fountain! Fill the buckets with water!"

The broom filled the buckets.

"Back down to the cellar! Pour the water into the well!"

The broom marched down the cellar steps and poured the water from the buckets into the well.

"Magic is easy!" laughed the apprentice. "I'll never have to work again!"

He sat down in the sorcerer's chair and put up his tired feet. *Y-a-w-n* . . . He watched the broom march up the steps . . . fill . . . down the steps . . . pour . . . up the steps . . . fill

. . . down the steps . . . pour . . . up the steps . . . *y-a-w-n* . . . and soon the apprentice was fast asleep.

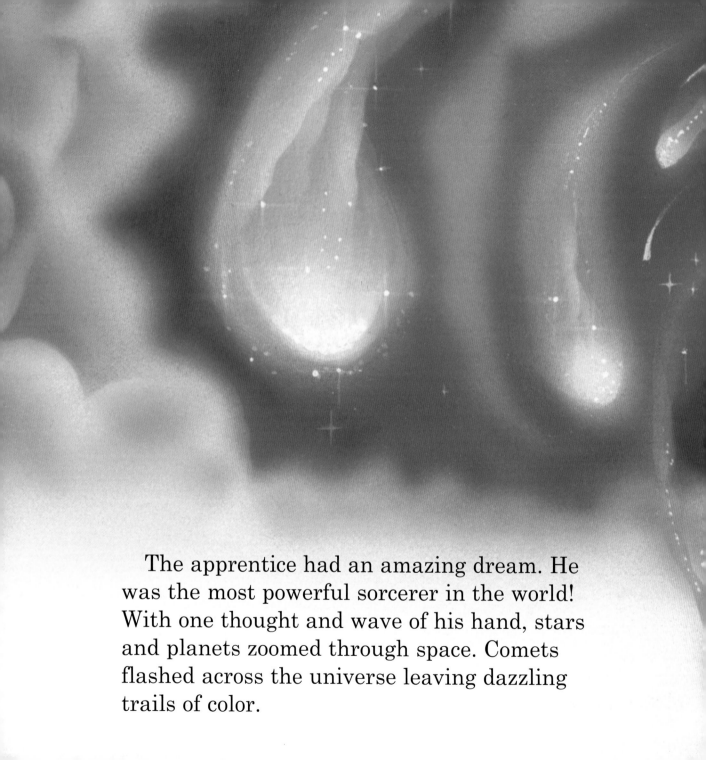

The apprentice had an amazing dream. He was the most powerful sorcerer in the world! With one thought and wave of his hand, stars and planets zoomed through space. Comets flashed across the universe leaving dazzling trails of color.

Up went his hands, and up went mighty waves in the ocean! The waves crashed all around him— higher and higher and higher, until suddenly . . .

. . . the apprentice awoke and found himself in a deep pool of water! The whole time he had been asleep, that broom had been marching up the steps . . . filling . . . down the steps . . . pouring . . . up the steps . . . filling . . . down the steps . . . pouring. The well was full and overflowing! The cellar was flooded!

The alarmed apprentice leaped up. "Stop!" he cried. "Stop, broom! Stop!"

But those were not the secret words to stop the magic. The broom did not stop! It carried on fetching the water.

The apprentice chased after the broom. He saw an axe up near the fountain, and he grabbed it. With all his might, he chopped that broom into hundreds of pieces.

"I've stopped it," he sighed, as he wearily turned toward the stairs.

But he was wrong.

Every piece of wood—every splinter, every sliver—began to move and grow!

Each piece became a new broom! Each broom grew two arms! Each arm picked up a bucket! And all those brooms marched straight toward the fountain to collect water.

The apprentice heard the noise, turned, and could not believe his eyes! He tried to stop the brooms, but they just knocked him down and walked right over him!

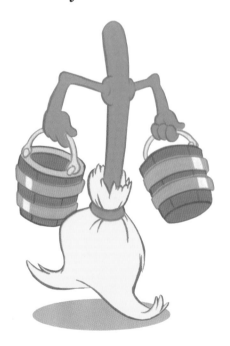

Like a great army, the brooms kept marching and marching. They tipped up their buckets, pouring more and more water into the overflowing well.

The water in the cellar rose higher and higher. The apprentice was swept into the water and struggled to stay afloat. When he saw the sorcerer's huge book of magic spells floating past, he jumped onto it.

Quickly, the apprentice turned the pages, searching for the special magic words. But the rushing water tossed him back and forth, up and down, and he could not read.

As he clung onto the book, the water became a mighty, swirling whirlpool. It carried him round and round, faster and faster.

The apprentice was terrified!

And then, there at the base of the steps, stood the
sorcerer. He knew at once what his apprentice had done.
Raising his arms, he ordered the water to disappear.

At his command, the water dried up and the brooms and the buckets vanished. Only the old broom and two buckets remained.

The sorcerer looked down with an angry scowl.

The little apprentice smiled and handed the sorcerer his magic hat. The sorcerer did not smile back.

The apprentice picked up his old buckets and tried to sneak away, but the sorcerer took up the broom and—w*hack!*—swatted the apprentice on the bottom.

The apprentice scurried off to do his work. He had learned his lesson: never start something that you don't know how to finish!